P9-CLO-102

Cara and the Wizard

To Flo and Iris — L. F.
For Delfina and Felipe, with love from Auntie Vale — V. D.

Barefoot Books
2067 Massachusetts Ave
Cambridge, MA 02140

Text copyright © 2013 by Liz Flanagan
Illustrations copyright © 2013 by Valeria Docampo
The moral rights of Liz Flanagan and Valeria Docampo
have been asserted

First published in the United States of America by Barefoot Books, Inc
in 2013. All rights reserved

Graphic design by Love Has No Logic Design Group, Chicago, IL
Color separation by B & P International, Hong Kong
Printed in China on 100% acid-free paper
This book was typeset in Albemarle, Bembo Infant
and Captain Kidd
The illustrations were prepared in
gouache paints and finished digitally

The editors would like to thank Year 2
at St. Mary and All Saints School for all
their careful reading.

Sources:
Nic Leodhas, Sorche. "The Lass
Who Went Out at the Cry of Dawn."
Thistle and Thyme. New York:
Holt, Rinehart and Winston, 1962.

ISBN 978-1-84686-780-4

Library of Congress Cataloging-in-Publication
Data is available under
LCCN 2012011234

1 3 5 7 9 8 6 4 2

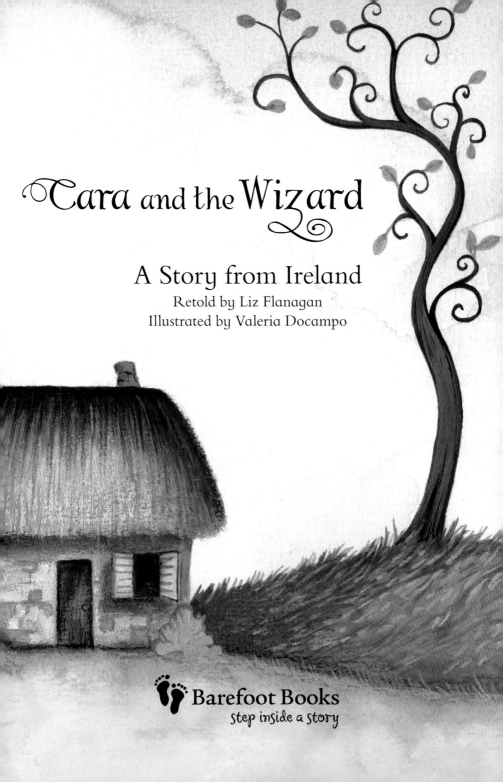

Cara and the Wizard

A Story from Ireland

Retold by Liz Flanagan
Illustrated by Valeria Docampo

Barefoot Books
step inside a story

CONTENTS

CHAPTER 1
The Two Sisters

Long ago in Ireland, there were two sisters called Molly and Cara. They loved each other very much. Day and night, they were always together.

But one morning, Molly went out alone. She went out at daybreak to wash her face in the morning dew. She did not come home again.

Molly's father looked everywhere for her. Nobody had seen her anywhere. Her mother cried for days.

Cara missed her sister terribly. Without
Molly, she was sad and lonely.

But Cara was brave — and clever too.
She said, "I will go out into the wide world.
I will look everywhere until I find Molly."

She asked her mother and father to wish her luck. Cara's father gave her his blessing and one gold coin. She put it in her purse.

"Take my blessing with you too," said Cara's mother. "And here are some gifts from me."

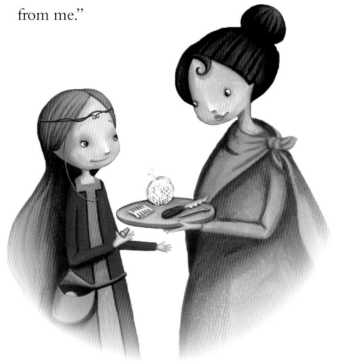

She gave Cara some pure white wool, a golden needle, a packet of pins, a sharp knife and a silver thimble. "Keep them safe until you need them," she told Cara.

Cara set off singing. She knew she had
to find Molly, and she was not going to
come home without her.

CHAPTER 2

The Cart with No Horse

Cara walked for days and days. She traveled many long miles.

One day, she met an old lady who told her, "There is a wicked wizard who lives in a castle at the top of that high hill. Maybe he has taken your sister away."

Cara walked to the bottom of the high
hill. It was very steep and covered in rocks.
She sat down to rest before she climbed it.

While Cara was resting, a man with a
cart came traveling past. He was a tinker.
He went from place to place selling his
kettles, cups, pots and pans. His cart was
stacked high with all sorts of things made
of metal. The cart went clink! clank! clink!
clank! as it traveled along the road.

But this tinker had no horse. Instead, he was pulling the cart himself.

So Cara called out, "That looks like hard work! Where is your horse?"

"It's hard work, sure enough," said the tinker. "But I have no money to buy a horse."

Cara saw that the tinker looked tired. She felt sorry for him. "Here, take my purse. I have one gold coin that my father gave me," she told him gently. "You need it more than I do. Go and buy yourself a horse."

The tinker's eyes sparkled with tears. "Thank you!" he said. "Nobody else will speak to me, but you have been very kind."

They sat down and talked together. The tinker asked Cara, "Where are you going all alone?"

Cara pointed to the castle, towering above them. "I'm going to look for my sister in the wizard's castle," she said.

The tinker tried to change her mind. He said, "Please don't go there! Many go into the castle, but no one comes out again."

Cara gave a shrug. "Molly is the only sister I have," she said. "I know there may be danger, but I must find her before I go home again."

So the tinker said, "I understand. You
are very brave, and your sister is lucky to
have you. So, if you must go there, please
remember this:

"Whatever you hear, whatever you see,
Things are never what they seem to be."

And off he went along the road. Clink!

Clank! Clink! Clank!

Cara started to climb the hill.

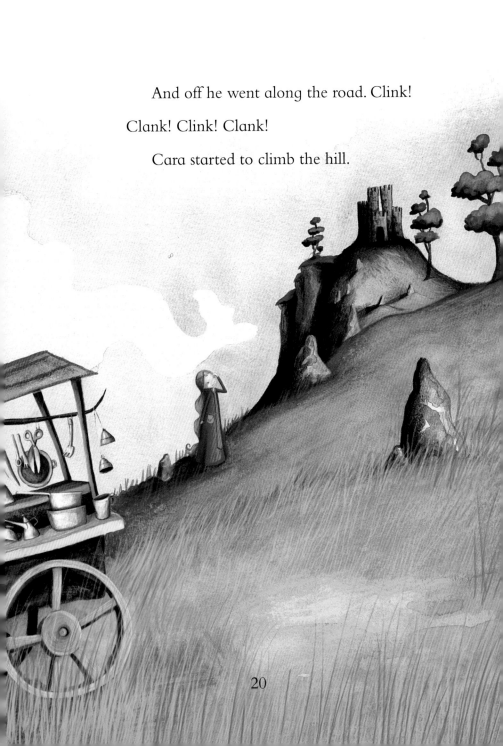

CHAPTER 3
The Ragged Old Man

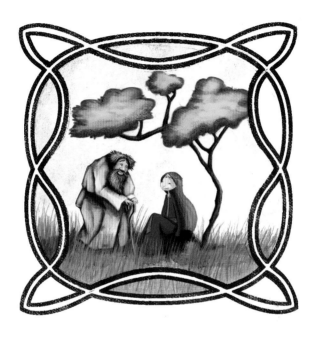

When Cara was halfway up the hill,
she sat down under a tree to rest. An old
man dressed in rags came walking past. His
clothes were falling apart. Cara saw that he
had pinned them together with thorns.

Cara said, "Hello! Would you like these
pins? My mother gave them to me. You
need them more than I do."

The old man smiled at Cara. "Thank
you!" he said. "No one else even looks at
me, but you have been very kind."

He sat down with Cara under the tree,
and they talked together.

The old man asked, "Where are you
going all alone?"

Cara pointed to the dark castle
above them. "I am going there to look
for my sister."

The old man begged Cara not to go
there. He said, "That old wizard is wicked.
He will cast a spell on you."

23

But Cara said, "I have to go. I must rescue my sister!"

So the old man said, "If you must go there, then remember this:

"Silver and gold will serve you well.
Silver and gold will break the spell."

Cara thanked the old man dressed in rags. She left him mending his clothes by the side of the road.

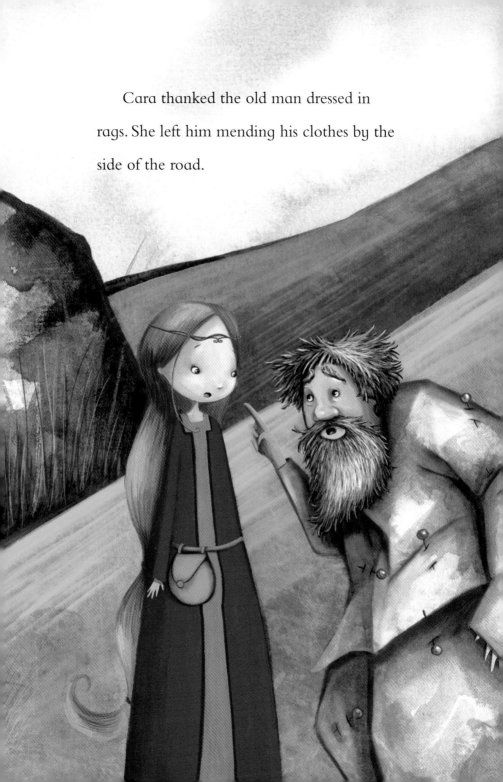

CHAPTER 4
The Wizard's Castle

At last, Cara climbed to the top of the
hill. She opened the heavy castle gates and
walked in. She marched up to the huge
front door and knocked loudly.

Suddenly, the wizard appeared next to Cara. He wore a swirling black cloak. His eyes were red, and his face was white. The wizard glared down at Cara.

"Who are you?" he growled. "Why do you come knocking on my door?"

Cara said, "I've come for my sister Molly.
I think she's here, and I want her back."

"Very well," said the wizard. "Follow me."

He took Cara to a room and left her there.

The room was empty. Cara could
not see Molly anywhere. She sat down
to wait. Suddenly, the room was
filled with smoke!

Flames crackled around Cara's feet.

The air was full of thick grey smoke.

"The castle is on fire!" Cara shouted.

She wanted to get up and run away.

Then she remembered what the
tinker had told her, and she
whispered the words to herself:

"Whatever you hear, whatever you see,
Things are never what they seem to be."

"This must be the wizard's magic,"
she thought. So she sat and waited.

Sure enough, the flames and the
smoke vanished all at once.

Next, Cara heard a sound that made her heart break. It was her sister's voice. "Cara! Help me! Please, help me!" Molly's voice begged.

Cara jumped up. She nearly ran to go and find Molly.

Just in time, she remembered the tinker's words again:

"Whatever you hear, whatever you see,
Things are never what they seem to be."

"This isn't real. It's only another spell," she said to herself. But her feet would not keep still while Molly's voice cried for her.

So Cara took the pure white wool that
her mother had given her, and she tied
herself to the chair.

At last, the voice stopped calling. Cara
took her sharp knife and cut herself free.

The wizard came back. He was very
angry when he saw that Cara was still there.

CHAPTER 5

The Hall of Statues

"Come with me," the wizard said to

Cara. He took her to a grand hall with high

windows. There was nothing in it except for

seven white statues. Each statue looked just

like Molly.

The wizard said to Cara, "If you can
tell me which one is your sister, then you
can both go free." He laughed nastily.

Cara walked slowly up and down and
looked at each statue. The wizard watched
from the other side of the great hall.

As she walked, Cara remembered what
the old man in rags had said:

"Silver and gold will serve you well.
Silver and gold will break the spell."

She took her silver thimble and put it on
the first statue's finger.

37

The silver thimble turned black as ink.

Cara knew this statue was not her sister. She

tried the thimble on the next statue. Again,

it went black. She did this six times.

Finally, Cara slipped the silver thimble onto the last statue's finger. This time it glowed with a dazzling bright light. The statue's white skin grew warm. Molly stood there, alive and well.

But Cara did not shout out. To trick

the wizard, she stood in front of Molly so he

could not see that her sister was alive again.

And then clever Cara pretended to weep.

The wizard laughed at her tears. While

he was laughing, Cara whispered to Molly,

"Quick! We must leave now."

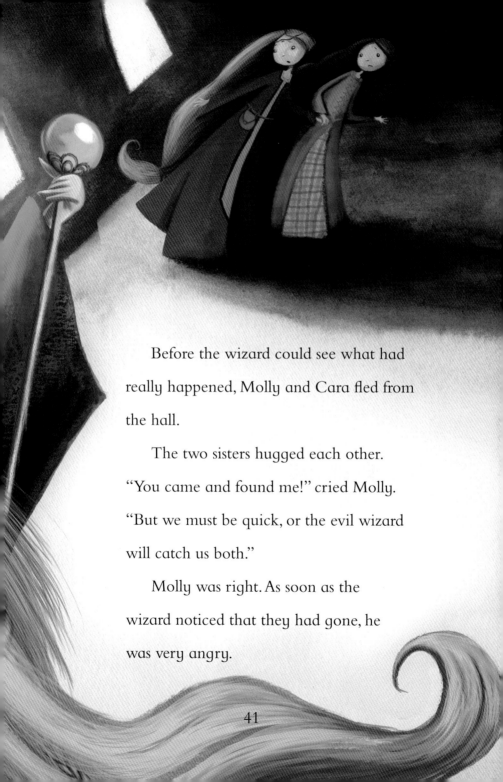

Before the wizard could see what had really happened, Molly and Cara fled from the hall.

The two sisters hugged each other. "You came and found me!" cried Molly. "But we must be quick, or the evil wizard will catch us both."

Molly was right. As soon as the wizard noticed that they had gone, he was very angry.

No one had ever escaped from the wizard before. He sent a huge wolf to chase after the sisters.

Cara and Molly ran fast, but the fierce wolf ran faster. It had nearly caught them, when Cara remembered what the old man in rags had said:

"Silver and gold will serve you well.
Silver and gold will break the spell."

She took out her golden needle. The wolf
jumped up at her, snarling and growling.
Bravely, Cara stabbed the wolf right between
the eyes. The wolf fell down dead at her feet.

The wizard was watching all this from
a tower at the top of his castle. When he
saw what Cara had done, he screeched
with rage. He flew after the sisters, his black
cloak flowing out behind him like wings.

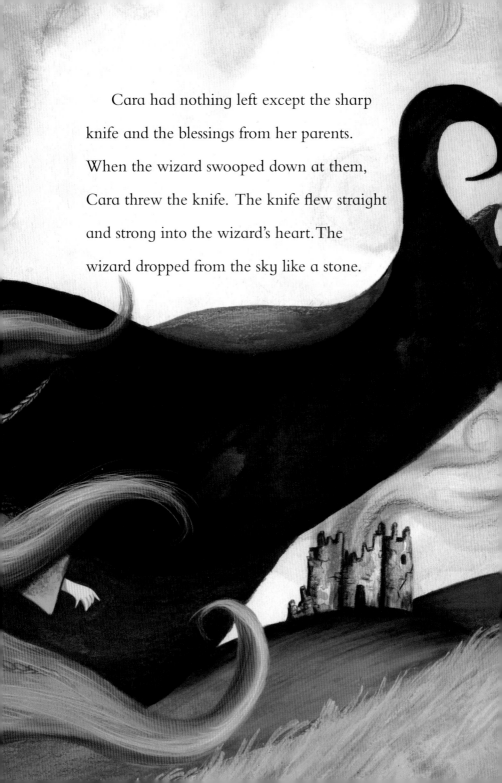

Cara had nothing left except the sharp knife and the blessings from her parents. When the wizard swooped down at them, Cara threw the knife. The knife flew straight and strong into the wizard's heart. The wizard dropped from the sky like a stone.

As soon as the wizard fell, his great castle crumbled into dust. All of his evil spells had been broken.

Cara and Molly walked slowly down the hill hand in hand. Halfway down, they saw a fine young man. He had Cara's pins in his hands. "I was the old man you helped," he said. "You have freed me from the wizard's spell."

At the bottom of the hill, they met
a handsome young man with a shining
coach. "I was the tinker with no horse," he
said. "You have freed me from the wizard's
terrible curse."

They all got into the coach and rode back to Molly and Cara's home. The sisters' mother and father wept for joy when they saw them.

Cara married the fine young man with the pins. Molly married the tinker with the shining coach.

They all lived happily together for the rest of their days. And the sisters were never parted again.